SHADOWMAN

Karen and Rob's show-jumping yard is in financial difficulties. And so is their marriage. Then someone starts sending nasty, anonymous letters. They seem to have an enemy who is determined to wreck their lives, but who? Is it a vindictive stranger or could it be someone closer to home . . . ? Karen is determined to find out before she loses everything she loves.

Books by Della Galton
in the Linford Romance Library:

NEVER LET GO

DELLA GALTON

---◆---

SHADOWMAN

Complete and Unabridged

LINFORD
Leicester

First published in Great Britain in 2004

First Linford Edition
published 2011

British Library CIP Data

Galton, Della
  Shadowman.- -(Linford romance library)
  1. Romantic suspense novels.
  2. Large type books.
  I. Title II. Series
  823.9'2–dc22

ISBN 978–1–4448–0847–6

Published by
F. A. Thorpe (Publishing)
Anstey, Leicestershire

Set by Words & Graphics Ltd.
Anstey, Leicestershire
Printed and bound in Great Britain by
T. J. International Ltd., Padstow, Cornwall

This book is printed on acid-free paper

It was a beautiful day. Autumn was just beginning to steal across the forest, turning the trees shades of red and gold, but I shivered as I leaned on the five-bar gate that separated our land from the tangle of woodland lying beyond. I had to talk to Rob again. Find a way to make him understand how worried I was; worried that if we didn't do something soon we were going to lose all that we'd worked for. It wasn't going to be easy. Rob and I didn't have the same attitude to money. I was used to having a nest-egg in the bank. I needed the cushion of financial security. Rob had an easy come, easy go attitude. To everything, I was beginning to think.

The differences between us hadn't been so apparent when we'd first married. But lately things had been tough financially. We'd had a couple of big bills that we hadn't budgeted for. Murphy, one of our horses, had been spooked by a backfiring car and had run into a barbed wire fence. The vet's bill had been horrendous and it had taken weeks of care to get him right again. Then we'd had a drainage problem in the stable yard and the builder had discovered subsidence, which had cost a fortune to sort out. We'd used our savings and now we were deep into our overdraft, and every time I raised the subject, Rob told me I was worrying too much.

'Things aren't that bad, Karen,' he said later that evening. 'The bank's hardly going to foreclose on us, is it?'

He smiled as he spoke, his eyes confident. There wasn't a trace of grey in his black hair, not a trace of worry, I thought ruefully.

'We can't just keep on borrowing. I think we ought to do something more positive.'

'Like what?' He raised his eyebrows

and I took a deep breath because he definitely wasn't going to like what I had in mind.

'We could sell a horse.'

'That's not going to make much difference.'

'It would if it was the right horse. Ben Darley phoned me this morning. He saw you riding Shadowman at Lulworth last week. He wants to buy him.'

'Does he?' Rob's eyes narrowed speculatively. 'What's he offering?'

I told him and he whistled. 'If he's that keen, then he obviously thinks the horse is going to be as good as I do. Excellent.'

'So you'll think about it?'

'No way. I'm not selling our best horse. It would be madness.'

I sighed and he came round the table and took my hands. 'Look at it this way, Karen. If Ben thinks he's worth that much now, then he'll be worth even more by the end of the season. I've got big plans for Shadowman.'

3

His eyes were sparkling, his face animated as it always was when he talked about the horse he'd reared from a gangly, long-legged foal, and I knew that I'd lost the battle, at least for now.

'It's going to be fine, Karen, I promise.' He went across the kitchen, dragged his coat from the back door and shrugged it on. 'Look, I'd better do the evening feeds. We'll talk some more later.'

I nodded, even though I knew that we wouldn't. Rob hated talking about money. It was ironic, really; Rob had been brought up with next to none and I'd always taken things like holiday homes, private schools and my own pony for granted, but I was the one who constantly worried about it.

The only thing Rob wasn't laid back about was his riding. He dreamed of being in the British show-jumping team one day and he was probably good enough to do it. The first time I'd seen him ride we'd been competing against each other in the same show-jumping class.

'That's the one you want to watch,' Mum had said, as we walked the course, and I'd looked at the tall, dark-haired man strolling ahead of us.

'I don't think I've seen him before. Who is he?'

'Rob Patterson. He's a bit of a rough diamond, but he can ride. He beat Suzy Canton last week effortlessly, if the rumour mill's to be believed. Caused quite a stir.' She patted her hair and raised her perfectly plucked eyebrows.

I hadn't taken much notice of the rough diamond bit — Mum's always been a snob — but I'd watched with growing interest as Rob jumped a perfect clear round.

He was an instinctive rider, so much a part of the horse that it had been breathtaking to watch him.

'Must have a good horse,' I'd murmured, but Mum shook her head.

'It's not his. Belongs to some small yard the other side of Salisbury. He'd never sat on its back until a week or so ago, apparently. The girl who normally rides it had a fall and couldn't jump today.'

I remember thinking that it must have been a lucky round, but that was before he beat me by a good ten seconds in the jump-off.

As we lined up to collect our rosettes, Rob grinned across at me. 'Nice mare you've got there,' he said, and I could feel myself softening beneath his gaze. 'See you again, I hope.'

And then he was gone, cantering ahead of me around the ring, and I thought, 'Oh yes, I'd very much like to see you again.' And not just on a horse.

A couple of weeks later we'd competed against each other again — he won that class, too — and this time he asked me to go for a celebration drink. That was how it had begun. We'd soon discovered that we were opposites in every way. Looks, backgrounds and personalities. I'd led a pretty sheltered life, really. I'd had relationships before Rob, but I'd never fallen in love, never wanted to get married. He'd said it was the same for him, but I wasn't so sure. Rob could have had his pick of women. Why had he chosen me?

Deep down, I'd always been afraid that it wouldn't last, that our differences would somehow drive a wedge between us, and I had a horrible feeling that it was beginning to happen.

★ ★ ★

Nothing's ever as bad in daylight as it seems in darkness, is it? As I crunched across the grass to check the horses' water troughs the following morning, I felt my spirits lift. Maybe Rob was right. Shadowman would certainly be worth a lot more if they had another good season, and there was no reason why they shouldn't.

Besides, it was hard to feel depressed out here in the crystal air. The first thick frost had silver-plated the grass, and villages of bejewelled spiders' webs sparkled in the hedgerows. The sun, which hadn't long risen, slanted across the fields, turning ice crystals to diamonds, so that it was easy to imagine you were walking through some winter fairyland, a place touched with magic instead of just our back field. I swallowed. I never wanted to leave this place. We *had* to make it work.

When the estate agent had shown us round two years ago, it had been a bright summer's day and we'd fallen in love with it. The house had needed a fair bit doing, but the stables were beautiful, a white-painted block that was big enough for twelve horses. We'd planned to offer a livery service and we were both qualified riding instructors. We knew it would be tight while we got established, but we thought we could make it work.

The house was on the edge of the New Forest and had only been in our price range because the owner wanted a quick sale, although I was well aware that we couldn't have afforded it had my parents not given us a hefty deposit as a wedding present and also acted as guarantors for our mortgage. This worried me, too, because neither of my parents had accepted Rob at first. I'd felt their unspoken disappointment that I could have done better. They'd come round eventually when they'd seen how serious I was about him. They'd trusted my judgment, both about Rob and my certainty that we could make a success of running our own yard. My parents were like that, but it meant I couldn't afford to let them down. Anyway, they couldn't help us financially any more, even if pride would have let me ask them. Dad's business hadn't been too good lately either.

I was on my way back to the stables when my mobile rang.

'Hi, Karen, it's Lynne. Any chance you could turn out my horses? Slight change of plan. I've got to go into work today. My boss has called some emergency meeting.'

'Is everything all right?'

'Yeah, well, I hope so.' Lynne

sounded distracted and I hung up, hoping that it was. Lynne was our best customer. We had three of her horses, all at full livery, which meant that she paid for us to look after them, although she exercised them herself when she had time.

Another reason that things had been a bit tight lately was because we weren't full. We only had six liveries. Rob had also been pretty busy with Shadowman this summer, going to shows most weekends, which took a lot of time out and was expensive. Even though they'd done well, it was mostly investment for the future, not real income.

At four, Lynne's Range Rover drew into the yard, and I smiled as she got out and came across.

'Hi! How's it going?' I said.

'Er, not too good, actually.' She brushed a hand through her immaculate blonde bob. 'Karen, I'm really sorry, but I'm afraid I've got some bad news.'

'Oh?' I felt a little shiver run through me.

'Yes, it's work. That meeting this morning was to tell us that the company has just been bought out. There are going to be quite a few redundancies, and some relocations. I'm one of the relocations. I've got to go to Leicester.'

I stared at her in horror. 'When?'

'Next month. It means I'm going to have to move the horses. I'm sorry.'

I touched her arm. 'Don't worry, it's not your fault. Are you OK? It must have been a huge shock.'

'It was.' She flushed and stared at the ground.

'When do you have to take them?'

'At the end of this week. I'll pay up to the end of the month, obviously. But I need to put things in motion.'

I wished I could tell her not to bother about the money, but I couldn't. Anyway, there was no point in pretending to Lynne. She was well aware of our financial problems because her father owned the feed merchants, who we always paid at the last possible minute.

11

'How are things here?'

'So-so.' I forced a smile. 'We'll manage. We always do.'

'I'll ask Dad to recommend you to his customers. You never know, you might get some replacements pretty quickly.'

★   ★   ★

Even Rob looked worried when I told him this latest development.

'We'll have to extend the overdraft,' he said. 'You can go to the bank — you can sweet talk Jack Dibbens any day.'

I booked an appointment for the following week, but I didn't feel in the slightest bit confident in my ability to sweet talk anyone as I walked into the branch. Jack Dibbens was young and very shrewd. He was going to see straight through my assurances that this was just a bad patch, especially as I wasn't sure what we were going to do about it.

He was as polite as ever, though. He pulled out a chair for me and offered me coffee and asked after Rob. Then he steepled his hands on the desk and gave me a steady look.

'Well, I think I can guess why you're here, Karen.'

Did I look that desperate? I felt myself redden under his steady gaze.

'We'd like to increase our overdraft. We've just lost our best livery owner, which has rather put us out. She had three horses with us.' I stopped gabbling, aware of his growing seriousness.

'I'd heard that things weren't going well,' he said at last.

I didn't answer. News travels like wildfire in our village. It was no surprise that he'd have heard that.

He looked at a sheet of paper on his desk. 'However, I'm prepared to let you go a bit deeper into the red, if you think it will help.'

'It will,' I murmured, feeling dizzy with relief. 'We are going to sort this out. I'm going to persuade Rob to sell a horse.' I told him about Shadowman and he listened, frowning.

Then to my surprise, he said, 'I think I'm with your husband on this one. Yards like yours are built on reputations. If you sell your best horse, you might find you've killed the golden goose, so to speak.'

I stared at him. I hadn't thought of it like that, and he smiled.

'Just a suggestion. Karen, there is something else I think you ought to know.' He produced an envelope from a drawer in his desk. 'The bank received this a couple of days ago. It was hand-delivered.'

I opened it and found a single piece of paper with a typed message.

The Pattersons are sinking fast. Even their livery owners are leaving. Can your bank afford to throw good money after bad?

It was signed *A well-wisher.*

Coldness spread through my stomach. It was hard to breathe. I met the bank manager's concerned eyes.

'If someone sent you this then why are you lending us more money?'

'I don't like being told what to do,' he

14

said simply, and held out his hand.
'Good luck, Karen.'

★ ★ ★

'I can't believe anyone would do this,'
Rob said. He was pacing the lounge, his
face creased with worry. 'It's obviously
someone who doesn't like us very
much. Who have we upset lately?'

'Plenty of people, if paying them late
counts,' I said wryly. 'But it's obviously
someone close if they knew about
Lynne.'

'Her firm's buyout was headline
news. Everyone would have known.'

'But not everyone would have known
she was moving her horses. Maybe we
should phone her and ask who she
told.'

He sighed. 'I'm afraid I haven't had a
very good day either. Shadowman
pulled a tendon earlier. I've had to call
Mike out to have a look.'

Mike was our vet. He was the best in
the area, but he was also the most expensive.

'Is it really necessary?'

'I wouldn't have called him if it wasn't.'

Silenced by the sharpness of his voice, I didn't reply, and he came across the room.

'I'm sorry. I'm stressed out. I didn't mean to snap at you.'

I looked into his eyes. 'It's all right. I know you didn't. We'll get through this, don't worry.'

He smiled ruefully. 'It makes a change for you to be saying that. But you're right. We will. Look, do you think you could deal with Mike when he comes? I'm going to go and see Lynne. I think we need to get to the bottom of this before whoever sent that note stirs up any more trouble.'

★　★　★

Mike might have been expensive, but he also had a brilliant bedside manner, if that's possible in a vet.

He crouched beside Shadowman in

16

his loose box and ran expert hands over the horse's legs. 'It's not serious. I've seen a lot of these lately. The ground's pretty hard.'

'How much do we owe you?' I said, when he stood up, brushing straw off his trousers.

'Don't worry about it. I was passing anyway.'

I glanced at him.

Had he heard about our financial difficulties, too?

He smiled, as if he'd read my mind. 'Karen, I wouldn't be much of a friend if I didn't do the odd favour, especially for you. And we are friends, aren't we?'

I nodded, feeling choked. Mike and I had been out together a few times before I'd met Rob. It had never been that serious, although my parents had been quite keen. I'd been almost thirty at the time and a vet had definitely fallen into the category of suitable husband. I think Mike had been pretty keen, too, although he'd seemed to take it well enough. Neither of us had ever mentioned it since.

'Thanks,' I said.

'My pleasure. How's Rob?' We stood outside Shadowman's stable in the afternoon sunlight and I watched Mike pack away his stuff, the sun picking out glints of gold in his fair hair. He was very attractive, not least because he was kind, and fleetingly a tiny, fickle part of me wondered what it would have been like if I'd married Mike instead of Rob.

'He's fine,' I said, blinking away the treacherous thought. 'And thanks, again.' And as I watched him walk away, it struck me that in times of trouble you found out who your friends were.

* * *

'So what did Lynne say?'

'Nothing. She wasn't in. I left a note asking her to call me.'

'But you've been gone for hours. I was about to phone round the hospitals.'

Rob frowned. 'I'm sorry. I should have phoned. I went to see an old

18

friend of mine. I thought I might be able to drum up a bit of business. Or at least get a few ideas on what we could do.'

'What friend?' I asked idly, not because I really wanted to know, but he'd been oddly quiet since he'd got back and I was worried about him.

'Tina Marsh. I used to ride for her. She runs a small yard in Devon. She's doing all right now, but I know she struggled when she first started out. I thought she might be able to give us some tips.'

'And did she?' I asked, still puzzled at his quietness.

'She said she'd keep an ear to the ground for anyone wanting liveries around our way. She also offered me some teaching work. She runs weekend seminars. They're quite well paid, so it'd be worth doing. Especially at this time of year.'

'Sounds like you had a successful afternoon, then.'

'You don't mind, do you?'

'Why should I?'

'No reason.' He grinned then and came and put his arms around me. 'What's for supper?'

While we ate we talked about Shadowman and I told him what Mr Dibbens had said about killing the golden goose.

'Smart man,' Rob said. 'And he's right, Shadowman is our best chance of staying in business. What did Mike say?'

I told him, trying not to feel guilty about what I'd been thinking about Mike, and perhaps he read something of this in my eyes, because afterwards he said, with unusual seriousness, 'You don't regret marrying me, do you?'

'Regret it — no, of course not. What's brought this on?'

He hesitated. 'You could have married some rich geezer, then you wouldn't have had to worry about money all the time.'

'I didn't want some rich geezer. I wanted you.'

'A bloke who had nothing but a dream of being a successful show-jumper and owning a half-decent horse. You could have done a lot better than me, Karen.'

'I married the man I loved. Who I still love,' I said passionately. 'Why? Do you regret marrying me?'

'No,' he said, less emphatically than I had and I looked at him and wondered if I'd been right. Had our money problems just highlighted the distance that was already growing between us? Perhaps he didn't love me as much as he once had. But I could read nothing in his eyes and I had the feeling he didn't want me to.

★ ★ ★

A fortnight later it seemed that our luck was starting to change. Tina had booked up Rob for three weekend seminars, one of them at the end of that week, and we'd had two calls about our vacant stables. Also, Ben Darley phoned again on Friday afternoon and increased his offer for Shadowman, which sent Rob dancing around the stable yard in delight.

'I don't know why you're so pleased when you've no intention of selling him,' I said, leaning on my pitchfork.

'Because it proves that I'm right. He's a brilliant horse and he's going to be worth a fortune by the end of this season. Ben Darley's no fool.'

Our farrier, who was banging a shoe into shape on his mobile anvil, nodded in agreement. 'Ben Darley's certainly no fool,' he muttered. 'Have you heard from Lynne lately? I bumped into her the other day. Shod one of her horses.'

I glanced at him in surprise. 'In Leicester? I didn't know you went that far.'

'I don't. She's at a yard on the other side of the forest. What made you think she'd gone to Leicester?'

'Because that's where she said she was going,' Rob said, frowning. 'That's where her job relocation was.'

'Must have changed her plans, then.'

'Strange,' Rob said, glancing at me. It was more than strange. Why on earth had she said she was going to Leicester and then moved just across the forest?

'I'll ring her,' I said, when the farrier was out of earshot.

'Did she ever return your call, Rob, about who she'd told about moving?'

'No,' he said tersely. 'She didn't. I would have phoned her again, but it slipped my mind. And I didn't think it was that important. Not now we've got the loan increased and the work with Tina. Which reminds me, it would probably be better if I stayed there tomorrow night. It's a long drive back and I'll be shattered from teaching all day.'

'Can we afford a hotel room?'

'Won't need one. I'll stay on Tina's sofa.' Seeing my startled expression, he slipped his arms around me. 'I won't if you don't want me to. But I thought you could probably manage the morning stables on your own, now that we've got so few.'

It wasn't the morning stables I was worried about, but I couldn't tell Rob this, not without sounding as though I didn't trust him. Anyway, I did trust him. Just because we'd had a few problems lately, it didn't mean he was going to go tearing off into another woman's arms.

'I can manage fine. I'll phone Lynne while you're away. Get to the bottom of this. I mean, if she moved her horses for any other reason, I'd like to know. And it is odd, isn't it? Especially with that letter that got sent to the bank.'

'Yes,' he said, his face shadowing. 'It is.'

He left the following morning with promises to call me that night and let me know how things had gone.

'You'll be too busy to miss me, anyway,' he'd said, grinning.

That was true, I thought, as I mucked out and rode our four horses. It was a bright October day, perfect for riding. At lunchtime I phoned Lynne. I decided to come straight to the point and ask her directly why she'd left us. There was a long pause . . .

'It's nothing personal,' she said eventually. 'And I wasn't lying about the job relocation, but it turned out that

I didn't need to go. I'd already given in my notice to you — and — well, I didn't want to mess you about.'

'But you wouldn't have been messing us about. Far from it. Have we done something to upset you, Lynne?'

'No.' Her voice was guarded. 'I just fancied a change of scenery, that's all. You know, different riding. You can get bored if you stay in one place for too long.'

'I see,' I said, although I didn't really. She was still riding in the forest, so it couldn't be that different. But she obviously wasn't going to tell me any more. Almost as an afterthought, I added, 'Did you tell anyone about your plans to move the horses?'

'Not that I can remember. Sorry, Karen, I've got to go. I'm a bit busy.'

And that was that. I put the phone down, bemused. Perhaps Rob could shed some more light on it. Perhaps Lynne had had an argument with one of the other liveries — or possibly even Rob. He could be pretty quick-tempered at times. But surely he'd have mentioned it.

I put it out of my mind and wondered how he was getting on. Mike had called by earlier to check up on Shadowman and I'd mentioned Rob was doing some seminars.

'And you don't mind?' he'd asked, a grin on his face.

'No, why should I?'

'Oh, no reason. Except that she's a quite a stunner, that Tina. Have you ever met her?'

I admitted that I hadn't and he shook his head, 'Well, far be it from me to criticise. You need trust in a relationship, that's for sure.'

'Yes, you do,' I said coldly and he stopped grinning and shut up.

All the same, I couldn't help thinking about what he'd said. Was that why Rob had acted so guiltily about the whole Tina thing?

He didn't sound in the least bit guilty when he phoned me up — quite the opposite.

'We've had a brilliant day,' he said. 'I'm going to have a couple of pints and then get my head down. How are things your end?'

'Not bad,' I said, and told him what Lynne had said.

'Oh, well, you win some, you lose some.'

'Don't you think it's odd? I mean, she must have had some reason for leaving that she doesn't want to tell us about.'

'Well, it's all a bit immaterial now.' He yawned. 'See you tomorrow, darling. Sleep tight.'

I had a bath and tried not to imagine Rob having a drink, or doing anything else with the stunning Tina. Then I went downstairs to check the back door was locked.

There was an envelope on the doormat. I bent to pick it up. No stamp, so it had been hand-delivered. My heart started to thump as I slit it open and pulled out a sheet of paper. It was typed, the same as the one that had been sent to the bank, but this one had

27

a different message.

First Lynne, now Tina — your husband can't keep his hands off the ladies, can he?

A well-wisher

I stared at it in shock. Someone must have delivered it while I'd been in the bath. Someone who was intent on causing trouble. My first instinct was to tear it into shreds, and then to phone Rob back and demand that he come home. But that was crazy. A phone call like that was going to cause a lot of trouble and may well lose him the job with Tina. Perhaps that was what the letter writer wanted. An image of Jack Dibbens' face came into my head and I heard his words again. 'I don't like being told what to do.'

I didn't either. I slipped the letter into my dressing-gown pocket, locked the back door and went upstairs. But I couldn't sleep. My mind churned over the possibilities. Why hadn't Lynne wanted to tell me the reasons she'd moved her horses? Could Rob have made a pass at her? Surely not.

I don't know what time I finally slept, but it was well into the small hours because, however much I thought things through, I kept coming back to the same conclusion. The first letter had been nasty, but it had also been true. What on earth was I going to do if this one was too?

I felt terrible when I got up for morning stables on Sunday. Worry and lack of sleep, I thought, as I prepared feeds and changed the horses' night rugs for day ones. My mind was still on the anonymous note and what I was going to say to Rob when he got home. I was tempted to throw it in the bin and say nothing at all. Not let the writer cause the damage that they'd obviously intended. But I wasn't sure if I had the strength of mind to do that. Besides, it would be worse if Rob found out about it at some later date. He'd wonder why I hadn't mentioned it. No, it was best to show him, give him the chance to explain.

I didn't want to admit that I was afraid of what he was going to say. First Lynne, now Tina, the letter writer had said. Well, all I knew about Tina was that she was stunning-looking, which wasn't very reassuring, but certainly didn't mean that Rob was attracted to her. He'd said they were old friends, which meant they'd been friends before we'd got married. And I was back in yesterday's cycle of insecurity. I hadn't exactly been inundated with offers before I'd met Rob, but it had been different for him. In the early days, he'd often joked that the horse world was full of predatory women. I snapped off my thoughts. If he'd wanted to go out with Tina, he'd had plenty of opportunities before. He wouldn't risk our marriage to do it now. I filled up hay nets and water buckets and decided I was being ridiculous; I was twisting myself into circles. I wouldn't be thinking any of this if the letter writer hadn't suggested it.

Mike had suggested it, too, I thought uneasily. Well, he hadn't actually said it in so many words. He'd just mentioned that you needed trust in a relationship. A throw away comment, that was all. I decided not to think about Tina. It was all too easy for my imagination to go into overdrive, but it was impossible to stop my thoughts drifting back to Lynne. She'd been with us since we'd started. She'd always seemed happy with the way we'd looked after her horses, but the fact remained that she'd moved them at short notice and she'd lied about why. It was very odd. I couldn't imagine Lynne being Rob's sort. She was older than him; a no-nonsense, practical sort of lady, and all she was interested in was working and competing. I didn't know much about her personal life; we'd never discussed anything much beyond horses. I didn't even know if she had a boyfriend. She wasn't the type of person who talked much about herself.

Rob got back just after ten. The Land Rover drew into the yard and he reached for his overnight bag and came across the yard, looking happy. There was nothing in his face to indicate that he wasn't pleased to see me.

'Hi, darling, how's it going?'

I waited for him to reach me, searching his face for tiredness, for clues that he'd been up all night.

'Is everything OK?' he murmured. 'Have you missed me?'

'Everything's fine and, of course I've missed you.'

He put down the bag and we hugged and I breathed in his familiar scent of aftershave and freshly showered skin and I felt my stomach muscles tighten. Whatever was I doing doubting him? I loved him so much and I didn't think he'd ever do anything to hurt me — yet I didn't mention the letter.

The chilliness of the morning gave way to sun, its warmth breaking through the clouds as we tacked up the first two horses we were exercising.

'Shall we ride out?' Rob asked and I nodded. Maybe it would be easier than talking here. At least there would be less risk of interruptions in the forest.

We rode along a path carpeted with fallen leaves, our horses' hooves thudding softly, the trees above us caught between summer and winter, their leaves half green and half gold.

'So you enjoyed yourself at Tina's then?' I asked idly as we came out of the woodland into the open where the bracken was beginning to turn rusty gold and clusters of New Forest ponies lifted their heads and cast curious glances at us.

'It made a change. It was nice to catch up.'

'Rob, if I ask you something, will you tell me the truth?'

'Of course.' He turned to look at me, a half frown on his face. 'What sort of something?'

'Were you and Tina ever more than friends? In the old days, I mean, before us.'

'No.' His voice was cold. 'We weren't.'

It wasn't the reaction I'd been expecting. I'd thought he might grin and say, 'Whatever gave you that idea?' Maybe even lightly accuse me of being jealous, but he obviously didn't want to discuss it. His shoulders were suddenly tense and, before I could say anything else, he pressed Shadowman into a canter and there was nothing else to do but follow.

When I caught up we were on the brow of the hill and Rob turned in his saddle, breathless. 'I'm supposed to be jumping Shadowman next weekend, but I thought I might give it a miss. He feels sound enough now, but I don't want to push my luck.'

'That's probably wise.'

He grinned. 'Heard any more about that girl who wanted us to look after her horse?'

'She's coming this afternoon to have a look round.'

'Well, that's good news. Our luck's on the upturn, don't you think?' I nodded.

'Well, don't look so fed up then. Come on, let's go back and get ourselves some lunch.'

★　★　★

The girl, whose name was Hannah, turned out to be blonde and pretty and my stomach gave a jealous little lurch when Rob said he'd show her round. I watched them walk across the yard, his head bent to tell her something, and I felt sick. This was ridiculous. Thanks to that letter I was beginning to suspect Rob of fancying every woman he spoke to. His reluctance to discuss Tina hadn't helped one bit. I decided I was going to have to take a more direct approach and show him the letter. But as it happened, I didn't have the chance. When I went in to the house, he was sitting at the kitchen table, reading it.

'Is this why you were asking me about Tina?' he said, as I stopped in my tracks when I realised what it was. He looked up at me, his eyes dark and angry, and I felt heat rush into my face. That note had been in my dressing-gown pocket. Surely he hadn't looked in there.

'Where did you find it?'

'It was on the bedroom floor. I was putting my stuff away. I thought it was something I'd dropped.'

'I was going to tell you. I was waiting for the right moment.'

'You think it's true, don't you? You're actually prepared to believe a letter written by someone who hasn't even got the guts to sign their name to it. For heaven's sake, Karen, I thought you trusted me.'

'I do,' I said, a mixture of guilt and pain sweeping through me.

'Not enough to tell me about this.' He screwed the note into a ball and hurled it across the kitchen.

'I'm sorry.' I was beside him in a moment, reaching for his hand, but he brushed my fingers away.

'When did it come?'

'Last night.'

'Who knew that I was going to Tina's? Who did you tell?'

I shrunk back at the anger in his voice. 'Rob, don't shout at me. I don't know. It was hardly a secret. Lots of

37

people, probably.'

'Well, I think we're going to have to be more specific than that. Make a list.'

'Where are you going?'

'Out,' he snapped and was gone before I had a chance to argue.

★ ★ ★

I made a list, but it wasn't very helpful. Anyone who'd been to the yard in the last fortnight would have known Rob was going to Tina's this weekend. This included the farrier, the feed merchant, my parents and any of Rob's pupils who'd been in for a jumping lesson. It probably also included most of the village because every time I'd done any shopping, I'd mentioned it, in a bid to quash any rumours that we were in financial dire straits. Stacks of people would have known. The only thing I was sure of was that it had been the same person who'd written to the bank.

I toyed with the idea of phoning Tina and asking her if she'd advertised the course at all, but I knew that this was just an excuse to find out what she sounded like. It wouldn't help anyway. I was hardly going to be able to tell if she was the type of woman who went around seducing other people's husbands simply by talking to her on the phone.

Rob came in just before tea. He looked tired and strained.

'I'm sorry,' he said. 'I didn't mean to fly off the handle earlier. It was a bit of a shock, that's all. I can't believe anyone would be so malicious.'

'It was a shock to me, too.' I paused. 'I've made a list, but I don't see how it's going to help us. Too many people knew.'

'Well, we could narrow it down a bit,' he said quietly. 'I wasn't completely honest with you earlier when I said there had never been anything between me and Tina.'

'What do you mean?' I could feel the hairs rising on the back of my neck.

'I did take her out a few times. It was before I met you and it wasn't serious.

It fizzled out after a few weeks.'

'Why didn't you tell me?'

'Because you wouldn't have been happy about me doing the seminars and we really needed the money.'

'You could have done the seminars without staying there the night.'

He shrugged. 'I could but it would have been exhausting. I didn't think it was a big deal. There's nothing between me and Tina now. I swear it. It's you who I married and it's you I love.'

I nodded, hating the fact that I wasn't completely sure if I believed him. Finding out that he'd lied to me, even if he'd thought it was a harmless lie, had rocked me. One more difference between us — because I'd never have lied to him. But I hadn't told him about the note, my conscience reminded me.

'The thing is,' he went on, immune to my silence. 'Whoever wrote that letter must have known that I used to take Tina out. That's why they picked Tina. They'd have known it would stir up trouble.'

'What about Lynne?'

He shook his head. 'That's complete fabrication. I've never laid a finger on Lynne. You have to believe me, Karen.'

'I'm going to go round and see her.'

'It's Sunday night. You can't go charging round and accusing her of having an affair with me. God knows what she'll think.'

'I'm not going to accuse her of anything. I'm just going to ask her why she really moved her horses.'

'Then leave it until tomorrow. We could both go.'

'OK. You're probably right. She might not be too impressed if we interrupt her Sunday evening.' I didn't add that I had no intention of letting him go with me. Although I wasn't planning on asking Lynne if she'd been having an affair with Rob, I had a feeling I'd get further if I went alone. And I wouldn't show her the note, but I thought I might take it with me. Just in case.

That Monday was a busy day for us.
Rob had morning and afternoon
lessons, the farrier was coming and
someone else phoned about our vacant
stable and asked if they could pop by
after work to look round.

'Perhaps it would be easier if I went
and saw Lynne on my own,' I said to
Rob. 'If we both go she might feel a bit
intimidated.'

He frowned and then he nodded. 'All
right. Can you pop into Mike's on your
way, do you think? We're out of
wormers.'

I was just leaving the vet's when
Mike came out into reception. 'Hi,
Karen, I thought I heard your voice.
Got time for a cuppa?'

I hesitated and he grinned. 'Come
on, you can't be in that much of a
hurry.'

It would have seemed rude to refuse,
especially after what he'd done for us
lately. I nodded and followed him

upstairs to his flat, which was above the practice. I watched him make coffee and, aware of my gaze, he turned. 'Is everything OK? How did Rob's seminar go?'

'Fine.' I took the proffered mug, cupping my hands around its warmth. 'It went very well.'

'You don't look very happy. Are you sure everything's all right? I'm glad you're here. I wanted to apologise, actually, for what I said the other day about Tina. It was thoughtless of me.' His voice was conversational, but his blue eyes were serious.

'Did you know they used to go out with each other?' I asked, meeting his gaze and hoping I sounded more casual than I felt.

'I had heard that, yes,' he said slowly. 'I wondered if he'd told you.'

'He told me last night when he got back.'

'I see.' He gestured to a chair. 'I wouldn't let it worry you. If he had anything to hide, he'd hardly have mentioned it, would he?'

'He mentioned it because he didn't have a choice,' I murmured, feeling guilty because it didn't feel quite right discussing my marriage with Mike, but he was a friend and one of the most discreet people that I knew, and I was sure it would go no further.

'What do you mean he didn't have a choice?'

I showed him the note and he read it and looked back at me, his eyes troubled. 'Oh, Karen, what a horrible thing to happen. Have you any idea who sent it?'

'None at all,' I said, even as something niggled at the back of my mind.

'If I were you, I'd ignore it. It's obviously someone out to cause trouble.'

'Well, they've succeeded,' I said wryly. 'And it's probably going to cause a bit more yet. I'm on my way to see Lynne.'

'You surely don't think this is true, though.'

'I don't know what I think at the moment.'

Before I could say anything else, he shifted his chair a little closer to mine and put his hand on my arm. 'Karen, you do know that if ever you need someone to talk to, I'm always here. I care about you. I always have.'

And suddenly I was very aware of him, of his touch, light, but proprietorial, of his eyes holding mine, and the stillness surrounding us. And I remembered how I'd once felt about him, but it was more than just the memory, because it was happening now. A little fizz of excitement. What would it be like if he was to lean a little closer and kiss me? I blinked and broke the gaze, broke the moment.

'Thanks,' I said. 'But I really ought to be going.' And then I stood up quickly before he could object. When I turned at the door, he was still sitting there, a half smile on his face.

I climbed into my car, feeling shaky. Perhaps this was how Rob had felt with

Tina; just one small step between friendship and infidelity. Good grief, I had to get a grip on myself. I loved Rob. Yet, just now I'd wanted Mike to kiss me. He'd wanted it, too. I'd seen it in his eyes.

It was only when I was pulling up outside Lynne's house that I remembered what had been niggling at the back of my mind. Well-wisher had known about our debt problems. He or she had known about Lynne moving her horses and also that Rob had once had a fling with Tina. Mike had known all of these things. It couldn't be Mike, I told myself, but unease crept through me as I waited for Lynne to answer her door.

'Oh, hello, Karen. I wasn't expecting to see you.'

'Can I come in? I need to talk to you.'

'What about?' Her face was guarded. 'I haven't got much time. I'm just on my way to do the horses.'

'It won't take long. Please,' I added,

because she looked as though she might refuse.

'OK.' She stepped back to let me pass. 'If this is about me moving, then I've really got nothing else to add to what I've already told you.'

'It's not about that.' We stood in her lounge eyeing each other like two wary cats. 'I'm really sorry to bother you, but I'm a bit worried about Rob.'

'Rob?' She looked surprised.

I nodded. It was clear that I'd get nowhere if I stuck to my original plan and asked her again why she'd moved. I decided just to show her the note. If it wasn't true, then she was likely to be as bemused as I was, and if it was I had a feeling that I'd be able to tell.

'I got this,' I said, and handed it to her. But her reaction was the last thing I expected. She laughed.

'What's so funny?'

'Is this some kind of a joke?'

'Not to me. Someone put it through our door.'

'You don't seriously think I've been

having an affair with Rob. I'm ten years older than he is. And he's not my type — nice as he is. For goodness' sake, Karen, you surely didn't come all the way over here to ask me that?'

'I didn't think you'd been having an affair, but I thought maybe he'd said something that got misconstrued, or flirted or something. I know what he's like. And maybe you'd taken offence.'

'It'd take a lot more than a bit of flirting to offend me.' She gave me back the note, still smiling.

'Then tell me the real reason why you moved your horses in such a hurry.'

'Ah, yes.' Her face shadowed. 'This is beginning to make sense. Well, It was nothing to do with Rob, I can tell you that.'

'Then why?'

She sighed. 'I promised I wouldn't say, but things are a bit different now, aren't they?'

I nodded, feeling my heart thumping uncomfortably, partly in relief and partly because I was sure I was on the brink of finding out the truth.

'I moved them because someone paid me to,' she said, perching on the edge of the sofa and giving me a direct look.

'I don't understand. Why on earth would someone pay you to leave our yard?'

'I must admit, I thought it was a bit odd at the time. In fact, I thought the guy was a total nutter the first time he asked.'

'What guy?'

'I'm not sure exactly who he was. I met him at a show. He looked like a groom. We got into conversation and he asked if I'd ever considered moving my horses to another yard. I said no, I hadn't, because I was perfectly happy with you.'

I nodded again. It was obvious that she was telling the truth. It was too bizarre a story to be made up.

'Anyway, I didn't think too much of it, but I saw him again a couple of weeks later and he asked if I'd had any more thoughts, and said that he highly recommended the yard he worked at and — well, to cut a long story short, he told me that if I moved I could get the first two months free.'

'So you went?'

'No, but I must admit I was tempted, Two free months for my lot was a heck of a lot of money. I took his card and said I'd call him if I changed my mind. Then that job relocation came up and I gave in my notice to you. And then I didn't end up going and it struck me that — well . . . ' She flushed. 'I'm sorry, Karen, I know it wasn't a very nice thing to do, but money's money at the end of the day.'

'Yes,' I said, because I was more amazed than cross with her. 'So, this guy works at your new yard, does he?'

'That's the curious thing. No, he doesn't.' When I went to see Anne Gates, who owns the place, and mentioned the special deal, she told me that my first two months had been paid upfront.'

'And you still don't know who the guy is?'

'No.'

'Did you keep his card?'

'Possibly. I'll have a look for you.' She disappeared and I waited, looking around her lounge, which was untidy and scattered with various items of horse paraphernalia, the walls dotted with pictures of her riding.

She came back in. 'There you go. It's a mobile so I'm not sure how much use it'll be.'

'Thanks.' I read the name, Keith Brown, which meant nothing to me.

'Do you know who he is?' Lynne asked, curious.

'No, but I'm going to find out.'

'He couldn't be the same person who wrote your note. That would be mad.'

Privately, I thought that paying someone to change livery yards was mad, but I didn't say anything. Maybe the two things weren't even linked, but I had a feeling they were unless, of course, there was more than one person who stood to gain something by destroying Rob and I.

I drove home, but my thoughts kept returning to Mike. He surely wouldn't do something like this. He'd seemed genuinely shocked when I'd showed him the note. And he was our friend.

'More *your* friend,' whispered a treacherous little voice in my head. Can ex-boyfriends ever really be friends?

Of course they can, I told the voice firmly, but I wasn't certain. The only thing I was sure of was that this wasn't going to go away. Sending notes was one thing; anyone with a malicious streak could do that. But paying someone hundreds of pounds was serious. Someone was out to destroy our marriage and all that we'd worked for, and they had to be obsessed to part with that sort of money. They might even be dangerous. And I was filled with a deep sense of foreboding because every instinct I had was telling me that they hadn't even started yet.

Rob was waiting impatiently when I got home. 'You've been ages,' he said. 'What happened?'

I told him what Lynne had said and he looked at me in amazement. Then he took Keith Brown's business card and studied it.

'So this man offered Lynne money to move her horses to another yard. That's insane.'

'He didn't actually give her any cash. He just paid Anne Gates for her first two months' livery.'

'I don't suppose Anne knows who he is either,' Rob muttered. 'Although it's worth asking her.' He was already turning, heading for the phone, when I put my hand on his arm.

'It might be better to go and see Anne.'

He nodded, but I could see he was

itching to do something. 'Yes, you're probably right. I'll phone Keith Brown, though — see what the bloke's got to say for himself.'

'You can't ask him outright.'

'No, I'll tell him I'm looking to move my horse to a new yard. See if I can find out where he works. Beyond that, I'll play it by ear.'

I waited, nervousness fluttering in my stomach. It couldn't be this easy. The guy hadn't exactly been straight with Lynne; he was bound to be suspicious of some stranger phoning him up. But then, I supposed, he wouldn't be expecting us to phone. He wouldn't even know we had his number.

Rob's expression changed and he slammed the phone down and cursed.

'What?'

'*The number you have dialled has not been recognised,*' he mimicked. 'Well, that's the end of that, then. I guess we're back to square one.'

'At least we know his name.'

'We know the name he gave Lynne. I

doubt very much if that's his real name. He probably got this card printed up especially.'

'We could still ask around. See if anyone's ever heard of him.'

'Yes, well, I suppose that's the only thing we are going to be able to do. Apart from speaking to Anne Gates. I'll go and see her tomorrow.' His face was etched with resignation, and I knew he thought, as I did, that discovering who was behind this, when they didn't want to be found, was going to be pretty tricky.

'Rob, I'm sorry. I didn't really believe there was any truth in that note about Tina and Lynne. It's just that this has all been so horrible.'

'It's OK.' He put an arm around my shoulders. 'In your shoes I'd probably have thought the same thing.' Then he smiled, but I could see that there was still a trace of hurt in his eyes. Words, once said, suspicions once aired, weren't so easy just to stick back in their boxes. If the letter writer didn't achieve anything else, he or she had certainly driven a wedge of doubt between us that was going to be hard to remove.

* * *

The following morning, while I was giving a riding lesson, Rob drove over to see Anne Gates. He came back looking frustrated.

'She's on a Caribbean cruise and won't be back until the end of November,' he said, tossing his car keys on to the work surface and running a hand through his black hair. 'She's obviously not short of cash, she's full up. I nosed about a bit and asked a couple of her girls if they knew anyone called Keith, but I drew a blank.'

'It's still worth speaking to her when she gets back. Why don't we just forget about it for now?'

'Guess we haven't got a lot of choice.' He touched my face, his fingers gentle. 'I'm jumping Shadowman at Woodfalls on Sunday and the other seminar that Tina booked me for is the weekend after. Would you prefer it if I cancelled?'

I hesitated. I was tempted, oh so tempted, to say yes. The last thing I wanted was Rob heading down to Devon to see Tina, especially now I knew they'd once been involved, but it was more important than ever that he knew I trusted him.

'We need the money, so no, I don't think you should cancel it.'

He nodded and I could see in his eyes that he knew exactly what I was thinking. 'I won't make use of her sofa, this time.'

'See how it goes, Rob. As you said, it's no big deal.' It cost me a lot to say that, but it was worth it, especially when he smiled in acknowledgement and kissed me gently.

* * *

Neither Rob nor I mentioned the weekend seminar again, although I couldn't quite dispel my unease about it. This one was for both days, so it really wasn't practical for Rob to drive back from Devon afterwards. I was doing my best not to think about it.

'I might come and watch you jumping tomorrow,' I said to Rob as we locked up the stables for the night. 'Would you mind?' I knew he was looking forward to showing off Shadowman, who was now fully recovered from his pulled tendon.

'Of course not, but are you sure the yard can spare both of us?'

'Quite sure. It's ages since I've watched you compete.' I patted Shadowman's dark bay neck and he dipped his head and snorted on my fingers. 'And I want to see how this fellow's doing.'

I was also still hopeful that I might bump into Keith Brown or somebody who knew him if I went to a few shows. Rob hadn't mentioned trying to track him down, but I wasn't going to give up quite so easily. Whatever else he had or hadn't done, Keith Brown had enticed away one of our best liveries and I was determined that he wasn't going to get away with it.

The day of the show was bright blue and frost-tinted and I felt my spirits lift as I mucked out stables while Rob groomed Shadowman until his bay coat shone.

'He certainly looks like a champion,' I murmured when a bit later on I watched him lead the horse, prancing and tossing his head, up the ramp of the horsebox.

'Shhh,' Rob said, looking anxious. 'Don't tempt fate.'

'Sorry.' I grinned at him. He was a brilliant rider but nerves always got the better of him before events. His olive skin was a shade paler than usual and he was as edgy as a kitten as he checked and rechecked that we'd got everything for the journey.

He seemed better as we drove, probably because he had something to concentrate on, I thought, glancing at him as we turned into the entrance of the show ground and bumped across the rutted field.

Their class wasn't until eleven so we had plenty of time before Rob had to walk the course or warm up Shadow-man. 'I'll go and get us some coffee,' he said and I nodded. This suited me fine. I was planning on doing a bit of sleuthing and he had enough to worry about already.

I gave him a couple of minutes and then I walked across the field towards the stewards' marquees, dodging past lorries and trailers, watching people leading out horses in bright rugs embossed with initials. A few riders were already warming up over the practice jump in preparation for the first class, and the breath of horses and their riders mingling was clouding the air like so much smoke. I listened to last-minute instructions being issued to anxious-faced competitors and the familiar sounds of leather creaking and the thud of hooves drumming on the hard ground. This had always been my life, I thought, breathing in the clear, sharp air and trying not to dwell on the fact that someone who was probably also intimately involved with horses wanted to wreck it.

There was a queue at the drinks van, but Rob wasn't in it. Perhaps he was picking up his number. I ducked under a guy rope and was just going towards the steward's tent when I caught sight of Rob up ahead of me talking to a petite girl in a riding jacket and jodhpurs. She had black hair that was twisted into a knot at the nape of her neck. They had their backs to me and I couldn't see their faces, but I knew instinctively that this was Tina. I stopped, torn between wanting to go over and introduce myself and worried that Rob might think I was checking up on him. I was also suddenly conscious of the fact that my own hair hadn't been near a hairdresser's for weeks and that I hadn't had time to put on make-up this morning. I turned and retraced my steps to the horsebox.

When Rob got back with our coffees a few minutes later, I was sitting in the cab reading a *Horse & Hound* and hoping it looked as if I hadn't moved.

'This should warm you up,' he said, handing me the polystyrene cup, his face flushed — from cold or from guilt I couldn't tell.

'Thanks. See anyone you know?'

'A few people.' He hesitated. 'Tina's here. I just bumped into her. I didn't know she was jumping today.'

'Oh, didn't you,' I thought, with a little twist of pain, because it had just struck me that his nervousness this morning might have had more to do with the prospect of her being here than normal stage fright. It might also explain why he'd been reluctant for me to come. But I swallowed down all this. I mustn't overreact. I mustn't let Well-wisher achieve what he or she had intended. At least Rob hadn't lied about seeing Tina here.

'I'll introduce you to her later,' he

said easily, sliding into the seat beside me. 'Bit nippy, isn't it?'

We walked the course together. Rob certainly wasn't edgy now, I thought, as we strolled round and he studied the angles and paced out a few of the gaps between jumps, his face a study of concentration.

'Which class is Tina in?' I asked.

'This one. I'm surprised she isn't here. Must have walked the course earlier. Pity, it would be good for you two to meet.'

I began to relax; surely he wouldn't have said that if there was anything going on between them? By the time it was Rob's turn to jump, I'd more or less convinced myself I was being paranoid. If Tina hadn't been so pretty, if Well-wisher hadn't suggested that Rob fancied her, then I wouldn't be feeling like this. At least that's what I kept telling myself.

'And next to jump is Rob Patterson on Shadowman.' The commentator's voice broke into my thoughts and I dragged my attention back to the present, watching them circling the ring in a perfectly balanced canter.

I'd forgotten how good Rob was. He hardly seemed to move on Shadowman's back. They just met fence after fence perfectly. Like clockwork, I thought, with a tug of pride. Even the commentator was impressed.

'A lovely clear round there from Rob Patterson,' he said approvingly. 'This little horse is turning into a real star.'

Rob was grinning as he rode out of the ring. 'Did you see that? Wasn't he brilliant?' He stroked Shadowman's neck and dismounted and the horse tossed his head and accepted all the praise as his due.

'It was an excellent round,' I said. 'Well done.'

'There are another eight to go before the jump-off so we won't hang around here and get cold. Do you still think we should sell him? Don't you think he's worth risking a bit of financial tight-roping for?'

'Yes, I think he is,' I said, looking at Rob's animated face. 'Has Tina jumped yet?'

'Haven't a clue. I haven't seen her again.' He gave me a look, half-curious, half-exasperated. 'Come on, let's take this fellow back for a walk round.'

There were five in the jump-off, Rob informed me, and he was in last. I stood watching the first competitor, a teenager on a grey horse, while he went to warm up Shadowman. It was a long time since I'd done much competing. I'd left it to Rob, who was more talented than I was, and I'd lost touch. I didn't recognise the next competitor either, but the third one in was Tina. Or at least it was the girl who'd been talking to Rob earlier.

'Tina Marsh riding Marsh Princess,' the commentator supplied helpfully and I felt myself tense as she cantered round. She looked even smaller on a horse than she had beside Rob. The sort of girl who should be a ballerina or an ice-skater, I thought uncharitably, not a husband-stealing show-jumper. Cross with myself because I had absolutely no grounds to base this on, I shook my head. Just because I'd seen them talking earlier, it didn't mean anything.

I was so engrossed in watching Tina that I didn't notice the man beside me until he spoke.

'Hello there. It's Karen Patterson, isn't it? How are things?'

I turned, startled, and found myself looking into brown eyes in a vaguely familiar face.

'Ben Darley,' he said, his smile friendly. 'We spoke on the phone. I was interested in buying a horse of yours, Shadowman. I still am.' Ben Darley had made more than one offer for Shadowman.

'He's not for sale.'

'Now that's a very great shame. I've had my eye on that horse for a long time.'

I glanced at him, surprised. 'Have you?'

'He was bred by an acquaintance of mine. As soon as I saw him I knew he was going to be good. And it looks as though I'm right. That horse will go a long way in the right hands. A very long way.'

'Rob's doing brilliantly with him,' I said, irritated at his implication that Shadow would be better with him.

'No one said he wasn't, but he'll have more opportunities in my yard.' He smiled disarmingly. 'If you'll reconsider, I'm prepared to up my offer.'

I looked at him, curious. 'If you were that keen, why didn't you buy him in the first place?'

'Because your husband gazumped me,' he said, his voice mild. 'I don't hold it against him. All's fair in love and war.' He glanced back into the ring. 'No one's jumped clear yet, so your husband's in with a chance. That course should be a doddle for them.'

Before I could reply to this, he nodded and walked away. He met Tina at the entrance of the ring and said something to her. Then they both glanced in my direction.

Feeling uncomfortable, I looked the other way and saw that Rob was heading across on Shadowman. He stopped beside me.

'Everything OK? I saw you talking to Ben.'

'Yes, it's fine. You just get in there and enjoy yourself. No one's clear yet.'

He grinned. 'We'll do our best.'

I watched them ride up to the steward, my fingers digging into my palms. Please let them do well. I wanted to see Ben Darley's expression if they won. Watch that arrogance slide off his face. No wonder Rob didn't want to sell Shadow to him.

Rob rode into the ring and I heard Tina call out, 'Good luck'. I didn't look at her. I concentrated on Rob, but I needn't have worried. He knew he had the advantage of going last. There was no need to rush things. All he needed was a clear round to win and he made it look so easy. They jumped faultlessly and he rode out of the ring to a smattering of applause and more enthusiastic acclaim from the commentator.

Adrenaline powered my steps as I ran across to meet him. 'Well done, darling. That was amazing. Really brilliant.'

'Thanks.' He looked thrilled. 'Don't rush off. You can meet Tina. I think she's in second or third place. Hey, we could all go for a celebration drink afterwards.'

'Shouldn't we get back?'

His face dropped and I could have kicked myself, but it was too late to say anything else because they were already being called back into the ring.

I watched as they collected their rosettes and prize money and then Rob led the victory canter around the ring.

When he came out, he dismounted and said, 'Perhaps you're right. We should get back. We'll leave you meeting Tina to another day when we've got a bit more time.'

I nodded, feeling a mixture of guilt

and relief, and wishing I hadn't said anything, because Tina was nowhere in sight anyway.

★ ★ ★

'I didn't know Ben Darley had tried to buy Shadowman when he was a foal,' I said idly as Rob and I mixed up the horses' evening feeds and refilled water buckets.

'Yes, he did, but I put in a better offer. He could have upped his, but he wasn't that keen.'

'You don't think he could have paid Lynne off, do you? Maybe he thinks he'll force our hand if we're strapped for cash.'

'It's a bit extreme, although I suppose it's possible. He wouldn't have sent those notes, though. Trying to hurt us financially is one thing, but trying to split us up is something else. No, I don't think that's Ben's style.' He frowned. 'I don't suppose you asked him if he knew Keith Brown?'

'No.'

I hadn't asked anyone in the end. I'd been too distracted over seeing Tina and Rob, but I wasn't about to confess to this. I'd done enough damage already by jumping to conclusions.

Rob switched off the yard lights. 'Come on, let's go in and get changed. I need a nice hot bath. You can join me if you fancy it.'

'Now there's an offer I can't refuse.'

We went into the house and all thoughts of hot baths and anything else for that matter were swept from my mind because there was a white envelope lying on the back door mat. We both spotted it at the same time.

'Another note?' Rob said, his voice half question, half statement.

'It looks like it might be,' I said, feeling my stomach start to churn as Rob bent to pick it up. 'Perhaps we should just throw it in the bin without opening it. We know it's not going to be pleasant. Why cause ourselves any more grief?'

'Because it might give us a clue to the sender,' Rob murmured, slitting open the envelope and sliding out the piece of paper. His face darkened as he read it, then he handed it over to me.

Shadowman's a valuable horse. But putting all your eggs in one basket is never a good plan for a businessman. Perhaps it would be better to sell him while he's still worth something.

A well-wisher

The piece of paper trembled in my fingers. 'Rob, this is a direct threat. We've got to do something. I think we should call the police.'

'What are they going to do? Send round a twenty-four hour guard — I don't think so. Anyway, it's not a threat. It's just worded to sound like one. It doesn't say they're going to do anything.'

'It implies it. At the very least it's illegal.' I hesitated. 'This has got to be something to do with Ben Darley. He's the only one who stands to gain anything by making us sell Shadow.'

'He's not that stupid. Anyway, he couldn't have delivered this. He was at the show with us.'

'He left before we did and he didn't have to drive back slowly in a horsebox.'

'It would have been too much of a risk. I said earlier that I didn't think it was him and I still don't. No, it's someone else who's got it in for us. Any ideas?'

'No,' I said, trying to suppress the niggling thought that Mike would have had plenty of time to deliver this note, and the look in his eyes the last time I'd seen him had been far from friendship, so maybe he had the motivation too.

'Me neither, but I'm not ignoring this. I think I'm going to move Shadowman.'

'Where to?'

'I don't know. Somewhere safe, just in case.'

'But we can't afford to pay for someone else to look after him, and what about his training?'

'I'll have to find somewhere cheap, somewhere I can still ride him. I don't know, maybe I could even go with him.'

'Rob, you can't. What about this place?' And I thought, but didn't say, 'What about me? What about my safety?' What would he do if he were given a direct choice? Would he take care of Shadowman or me? I suppressed a little shiver because, as I looked back into his intense eyes, I had to admit that I was no longer sure.

Rob was up before me the following day. I couldn't hear him moving around downstairs and he didn't bring me my normal breakfast cup of tea. The space beside me was cold and I wondered how long he'd been gone. It wouldn't have surprised me a bit if he'd spent the night in the stable guarding his beloved horse. But then, after yesterday's note, I couldn't have blamed him. I found him in the yard. He'd already done the morning feeds and was standing by Shadowman's box. The bay horse looked fine, I saw with relief, as I went across.

Rob turned, yawning. 'Hi, love, I couldn't sleep so I thought I'd make an early start.'

'Have you thought any more about what we're going to do?'

'I've thought of nothing else.' He

frowned, lines of tiredness around his eyes. 'I think we are going to have to move him. As you say, we can't afford to pay for his livery, but I think I've got a solution.'

'Tell me,' I said, even though I had a feeling I knew exactly what was coming.

'I'm going to ask Tina. I'm pretty sure she wouldn't mind, if I explained what was going on. I'm going down there next weekend, anyway, but it might be best if I took Shadow down sooner than that. I really don't want to take any risks.'

I hesitated. It was beginning to look as though every way that we turned we were taking risks. With our business, with our horse, maybe even with our marriage, but I was also very aware that we were fast running out of options.

'What will you do about paying her?'

'I've thought about that, too, I could suggest that I do a couple of extra courses for her, free of charge — but actually I don't think she'll mind at all in the circumstances. She's nice. You two would get on well.'

'I'd like to meet her. We didn't get much chance at the show.' I hoped I sounded more enthusiastic than I felt.

'I'll phone her later and run it by her. See what she says. In the meantime, I think we ought to have a serious think about who our mystery note writer could be. It's got to be someone close.'

I nodded in agreement, shivering slightly in the early morning chill. He was right, moving Shadowman could only be a temporary solution. We had to find out who Well-wisher was and we had to find out soon.

★ ★ ★

I've always been the type of person who can think better if they're doing something. I wasn't teaching that day, which meant I was exercising all the horses that needed it. I rode two of them and lunged the other one in the paddock, keeping him circling round me on the long line, my movements automatic, while I let my mind roam over the possibilities.

Rob was right; it had to be someone we knew. Well-wisher was too well-acquainted with our movements to be that far away. I knew Rob didn't think it was Ben Darley, but I wasn't so sure. The note writer must have something to gain by splitting us up or closing us down, which, practically speaking, amounted to much the same thing. Ben was the only one I could think of who did. Apart from Mike, of course, but I still didn't want to think that this had anything to do with him.

I decided that I was thinking too logically. Perhaps there was someone who had some reason I just didn't know about. I thought about all the people who'd come into the yard in the last few weeks. The farrier, but he surely wouldn't want to put us out of business, quite the opposite. The feed merchant came regularly, but he was Lynne's father and I could see no reason why he'd pay his own daughter to move her horses.

Obviously, there were our other liveries. Kathy was a nurse who worked long hours and mostly rode at weekends, and the other two horses we had both belonged to teenagers who came in most days. I discounted the possibility of it being any of them. The only real clue we had so far was the name Keith Brown and I agreed with Rob that this probably wasn't even a real name, but it was time we made a serious effort to track him down.

Rob and I met up at lunchtime when we went indoors for a sandwich.

'I've spoken to Tina, and she's fine about having Shadowman.' He grinned. 'I knew she wouldn't mind.'

'When did you say you'd go?'

'Well, I didn't, but I thought maybe this afternoon. No sense in hanging around.'

'But there's so much to do. Mike's coming in to do the flu jabs. In fact, he should have been here by now. The farrier's due at three and you've got your lessons. And my parents are supposed to be coming by later. We haven't seen them for ages.'

Rob frowned. 'Ah yes, I'd completely forgotten that they were coming.'

That didn't surprise me in the slightest. Although Rob got on with my parents a lot better than he had when we'd first married, there was still a bit of awkwardness between them, which was one of the reasons we didn't see so much of them these days.

He shrugged. 'Well, it's entirely up to you, but I really don't suppose your parents will mind if I'm not here. It's you they really want to see.' His voice was suddenly hard and I looked at him in concern.

'That's not true, Rob. They like you . . .'

A rap on the back door stopped me in mid-sentence and then Mike came in without waiting for an answer.

'Sorry to burst in on you guys, but I've got a bit of an emergency.'

'Emergency? Well, if you need to

leave the jabs that's fine by us. We were just saying, we're pretty busy.'

Mike shook his head impatiently. 'I've done them. Kathy said you were having your lunch. 'No, I'm afraid it's Shadowman. He's got colic.'

'He's what?' Rob leapt to his feet. 'He was fine earlier.'

'Well, he's not now. I spotted him in the field, about to roll, and he didn't look quite right. I've brought him in and I've dosed him, but he'll need an eye kept on him. It's a good job I called round when I did.'

Rob, his face pale, was already heading for the door, but I was slower. I stared at Mike in shock. All I could think about was last night's note. It had been a direct threat to Shadowman. And now he had colic. Fear slipped down my spine. 'Mike, is there any way you can give a horse colic?'

He must have caught the urgency in my voice because he came across the kitchen.

'Well, yes, there are a few things you

could do that might bring it on, but you surely don't think anyone did this on purpose? Horses get colic all the time and you were competing yesterday, weren't you? It could well be something to do with that.'

I stood up. My legs felt rubbery. I hadn't taken the last note as seriously as Rob had. I hadn't believed that anyone would truly try to hurt our horse. I'd been trying to talk him out of going today and now Shadowman was ill.

'Karen, are you all right?' I was aware that Mike was looking at me, his face troubled. 'What's going on?'

'We had another note,' I said, 'but I didn't think it was really going to happen. Someone threatened to hurt Shadowman.'

'When?'

'Last night. We were going to move him this afternoon.'

'You're not going to be able to move him anywhere for a while.' He stepped closer and put his hands on my shoulders. 'You're trembling and you're as white as a sheet. Sit down a minute. Rob will be fine. He knows what to do.'

I did as he said, and rested my head in my hands. He was right; I felt giddy and sick.

I heard the scrape of chair legs as he sat beside me. 'I don't think anyone's done this on purpose, I really don't. It's just one of those things.'

'It's a bit of a coincidence, though, don't you think?' My hands felt clammy in my lap.

'He'll be fine. To be honest I'm more worried about you,' Mike said evenly, and when I eventually looked up, I could see that he meant it. Deep concern was etched on his face. 'All this is getting to you and you can't let it. You'll make yourself ill.'

I was close to tears, as much from the kindness in his voice as from the shock of what had just happened. It was a few moments before I could speak and Mike just sat, his solid presence very comforting, while I got myself together.

The silence settled around us.

'Feeling better?' he asked eventually. 'You're a better colour, anyway.'

'Yes, I'm fine.' I looked at him. 'Thanks so much, Mike. I'm really glad you were here.'

'Any time,' he said, giving me a wry half-smile. 'I'll take one more look at him before I go but, as I said, he's going to be fine. You take care of yourself. And remember what I said — if ever you want to talk, you know where I am.'

The back door slammed behind him, but for a while I stayed where I was. I was so glad I hadn't mentioned my suspicions about Mike to Rob. Colic could come on so quickly, could be fatal if it wasn't caught in time, and I shuddered to think of what could have happened if we hadn't noticed.

★ ★ ★

Shadowman was fine, as Mike had said he'd be, but that didn't stop Rob fretting.

84

'Mike didn't give you any clue as to what he'd thought caused this, did he?' he asked, as we stood at Shadowman's stable just before sunset, watching him pull at his hay net.

I shook my head. 'He didn't seem to think it was deliberate.'

'No, that's what he told me. I'm not so sure. Who's been in here today?'

'Only the livery owners. It was pretty quiet this morning.'

'And it's not very likely to be any of them,' he said, echoing my thoughts. 'Karen, this is doing my head in. I think it would be a good plan if I took Shadowman down to Tina's tonight.'

'But Mike said we shouldn't move him.'

'I think it's riskier leaving him here. Look, I'll go. I'll take it really steady and I can stop and check him every so often. Maybe if you phoned your parents and talked to them, they'd stay over. I'm sure they would.'

Yes, I was sure they would, too, and although I wasn't thrilled at the prospect of him heading off to Tina's for the night again, I knew that it was about time I got things in perspective.

'All right. I'll call them and ask if they'll stay over.'

Mum agreed straight away, even though I said I couldn't tell her the whole story on the phone. I would get the full interrogation when they arrived, I thought wryly. Mum would be jumping to all sorts of conclusions by now. She'd probably think Rob and I had argued. We'd seen less and less of them lately, even though they lived barely twenty miles away.

'Rob doesn't want us over every five minutes,' Mum had said the last time I'd mentioned it, but I'd had the feeling that there was more to it than that. My parents were old-fashioned and I suspected that while they'd accepted Rob on the surface, they would never be totally happy that I'd married someone who hadn't been brought up with the same advantages I'd had. They were too polite to show this, but Rob was as sensitive as radar and I knew the unease went both ways.

I didn't want to acknowledge that there was a part of me that was beginning to think my parents might be right. Would I have felt the same unease if there hadn't been so many differences between us? Not that I was going to admit this to my parents; it would have felt like a betrayal.

When Rob had left, after insisting that I lock all the doors and windows, I wandered around the house and hoped they wouldn't be too long. The house felt empty without Rob in it and, although we weren't exactly miles from civilisation, our nearest neighbour was a good mile away and I felt very alone.

The doorbell rang bang on eight and I let them in. My father smelled of pipe tobacco and Mum smelled of expensive cologne, which took me straight back to childhood.

'Go and put the kettle on, Stephen,' Mum said, as soon as I'd taken their coats. 'Karen and I have got a lot to catch up on.'

She drew me on to the sofa beside her. 'We're very worried about you, darling. You sounded awful on the phone earlier. Are you and Rob having problems? He hasn't moved out permanently, has he?'

Typical Mum, I thought. No beating about the bush. 'Of course he hasn't and, yes, we are having problems, but not in the way that you think.'

'Something's obviously wrong and in my experience only two things cause problems in a marriage; money or another woman.'

I smiled despite myself. 'It's more complicated than that. And you can tell Dad he can come in. I'd quite like him to hear this.'

Her eyebrows lifted in puzzlement, but she did as I said. Actually, it was a relief to pour it all out to them. My parents might not have a lot of faith in Rob but they were kind and they were practical, and it was infinitely reassuring having them with me.

'My guess is it's this Ben Darley chap,' Dad said from the corner of the room where he was standing with his hands clasped behind him. 'He's got the money and he's got the motivation.'

'Because he wants to buy Shadow-man?'

'Because your Rob snatched the horse from under his nose. It'll be a revenge thing. Why don't you go round and see him?'

'She can't just confront him,' Mum said, throwing him an impatient glance. 'Anyway, I'm not so sure you're right. He couldn't have given the horse colic. He wasn't here.'

'Probably paid someone to do it,' Dad said stubbornly.

'You've been watching too many *Midsomer Murders*, Stephen.' Lines creased her forehead. 'What did you say the man's name was — the one who bribed your livery away?'

'Keith Brown — why, do you know who he is?'

'Something's ringing a bell. Give me a minute. Something from a long time ago. It'll come to me.'

Dad stuck his hands in his pockets and looked sceptical, but I was more hopeful. Mum wasn't involved in horses much these days, but she'd been very involved when I was younger, at least on the social side, and the circuit didn't change all that much.

'Got it,' she said, clapping her hands together. 'He used to work for that nice vet. The one you dated for a time. What's his name?'

'Mike,' I said, feeling coldness creeping through my stomach. 'He's still our vet. He was here today, in fact.'

'I've never heard such rubbish in my life,' Dad said. 'He's a damn good fellow, that Mike. He wouldn't be caught up in something like this.'

'No,' Mum agreed slowly, 'I don't suppose he would. But I'm sure I've got the name right. It was about five or six years ago that Brown worked at the practice. You could always ask Mike if he knows where he went.'

I looked from one to another of their faces and wondered if I should tell them that I'd been trying to convince myself for days that it had nothing to do with Mike. I decided against it. It would open up a whole new can of worms and it was late, and however much everything seemed to point in Mike's direction, I couldn't bring myself to put my suspicions into words.

'I'll ask him tomorrow,' I murmured. 'Thanks, Mum. At least we're a bit further ahead than we were.'

We went to bed soon afterwards. My parents always went early and I was tired from worrying. I fell asleep, a little anxious because I'd been expecting Rob to phone and he hadn't.

Mum cooked me breakfast the following morning. 'I've been thinking, Karen,' she said, as she ushered me into a chair. 'Your livery owner, Lynne, might have been lying about someone paying her to move her horses. I think I'd be tempted to go and see her again if you don't get any further with this Keith Brown character.'

'Yes,' I said, eyeing with alarm the mountainous breakfast she was pushing towards me.

'And I know you're not going to want to hear this, but I also think you should have a serious talk with Rob. I don't think it's very responsible of him to go flying off and abandoning you in times of trouble.'

'He hasn't abandoned me. He's protecting our best horse.'

'Well, it isn't right. He should be looking after you. How are the two of you getting on — generally, I mean?' Her voice was ultra casual.

'We're fine.'

'So you won't be wanting us to stay another night?'

'No, he'll be back later,' I said, hoping I was right because he hadn't actually said. I'd been expecting him to tell me when he'd phoned. I'd call him as soon as my parents had gone, I decided.

I waved them off after breakfast.

'Let us know how you get on with Mike,' Mum called. 'And do let us know if you'd like us to come back tonight. It's really no trouble.'

It was very quiet when they'd gone. I phoned Rob and discovered his mobile was switched off, so I hunted frantically for Tina's number and realised I didn't have it. I still wasn't unduly worried. It was only just gone nine; Rob would assume I was out in the stables and the signal was always bad there. Or was I making excuses for him? To prove that I wasn't, I decided to go down to the bottom field on the farthest edges of our land and clear the manure. It hadn't been done for a couple of days and, although it wasn't the nicest of jobs, I found it quite relaxing wandering about with my wheelbarrow and a shovel. As I worked, I thought about Mike and what I was going to say to him.

I was just straightening up and about to go and empty the wheelbarrow when

I saw someone moving along the fence line just up ahead of me. The sun was in my eyes and I shielded them. A man carrying a bucket. How very peculiar.

'Hey,' I called. 'You're trespassing.'

The figure turned and I saw with a little jolt that it was Mike. What on earth was he doing in our field?

He came towards me and, as he got closer, I could see that he was flushed and out of breath. I waited until he stopped in front of me. There were apples in the bucket, little green apples, some of them starting to rot, and as I glanced around I could see that there were others scattered about. Rotting apples could give a horse colic faster than anything else and there shouldn't be any in our field. We always made sure of that.

I stared at him in horror and I could see by his expression that he knew exactly what I was thinking. There could be no pretending, no talking my way out of this one. His face went an even deeper red and his eyes, usually so friendly, were icy cold. For a moment I couldn't move. I was up here, alone with him, with a mobile with no signal, and I was suddenly terribly afraid.

I swallowed down my fear and took a deep breath. Why hadn't I listened to the inner voice that had been telling me that Mike had something to do with this all along? If I'd trusted my instincts, Rob wouldn't be in Devon and I wouldn't be face to face with Well-wisher, the person who'd tried to destroy us; Mike, the man I'd thought was one of our closest friends.

But before I could gather my thoughts enough to speak, Mike shook his head, his eyes still icy. 'You think I did this, don't you, Karen? You actually think that I'd try to poison your horse. I'm a vet, for God's sake, not some sort of sick pervert.'

He was bound to try to talk his way out of it. I kept my voice steady. 'Then what are you doing with that bucket?'

'You told me yesterday that you

thought someone had deliberately given Shadowman colic. It struck me this morning that if they had, this might be a good way to do it.'

'Apples?' I raised my eyebrows in disbelief.

'I didn't know it was apples — but I figured it was worth having a look. He was turned out in this field yesterday, wasn't he? I was passing so I stopped.' He put the bucket down. 'I wish I hadn't now. I thought you trusted me. I thought we were friends. I can see I was wrong.'

He held my gaze and I struggled with myself. He sounded so sincere, but there was too much stacked against him. Keith Brown's card was still on our kitchen table. Keith Brown had once worked for Mike. It was simply too much of a coincidence.

'I think it's best if you get yourself another vet,' Mike continued with a thread of bitterness in his voice. 'One you *do* trust.' He turned and began to head back the way he'd come.

I went after him. 'Mike, wait. Look,

we can't leave things like this. Please will you come into the house for a minute? There's something I have to ask you.'

A second's hesitation and then he nodded. We walked back across the field, a slight distance between us, and my heart thumped uncomfortably. I knew I was taking a risk by asking him to come into the house while there was no one else about, but I no longer cared. Either he was involved or I had just done him a terrible disservice. I had to find out which.

★   ★   ★

Mike refused my offer of coffee and stood in the kitchen with his hands in his pockets. 'I can appreciate that you've been under a lot of stress lately, but it would be nice to know what you think I'd have to gain by trying to cause trouble between you and Rob — not to mention attacking your horse.'

I didn't answer. I could feel my face

flaming. This was going to be harder than I'd thought. He was looking at me, puzzlement in his eyes, and then I saw dawning realisation creep across his face as he worked it out.

'You think I'm jealous because you dumped me and married him? That's it, isn't it?'

I didn't say anything. His voice was so incredulous that I knew I'd got that completely wrong.

'It wasn't just that.' I showed him Keith Brown's card. 'This man paid Lynne to move her horses. He's involved with all this and he used to work for you, didn't he?'

He nodded and looked back at me. 'OK, I admit that I had hoped things would work out differently between us, but I could see how you felt about Rob and I accepted it. I had no choice. Although, if I hadn't been sure that he loved you as much as you loved him, I might have kicked up more of a fuss.'

It was plain that he was telling the truth.

'I'm so sorry, Mike. I've jumped to all the wrong conclusions.'

'Well, I'm beginning to see why. But I'd never have tried to hurt you. Or Shadowman.' He smiled ruefully. 'I didn't pick a very good time to collect apples, did I?'

He picked up the card and turned it over in his hands. 'Why didn't you just phone Keith?'

'We tried, but the number didn't work. He must have changed it.'

Mike frowned. 'He jacked in the idea of a career in veterinary practice, but he still works with horses. The last time I heard anything about him, he was working for Ben Darley.'

I stared at him in shock. 'It's got to be him,' I said, feeling hollow.

'I can't understand why he'd want to give him colic either. It just doesn't make much sense, does it?'

'No, but it has to be him. It all fits.'

'You thought it was me about ten minutes ago.'

'That's true.' I smiled at him

uncertainly, amazed that we were sitting here having this conversation. 'I'm so sorry about that.'

'Forget it. I'm getting less surprised by the second, to be honest. But I don't think you should go rushing round to Ben's accusing him of anything. At least, not on your own.'

'Will you come with me?'

'Much as I'd like to play the hero, I don't think that's a very good idea. It's Rob who should go with you, not me.'

'Rob would kill him. And, anyway, he isn't here.' I told him about Rob's decision to take Shadowman to Tina's the previous night. 'He hasn't rung me yet,' I said, glancing across at the answer phone, and seeing that he hadn't left a message. 'I'm really worried.'

'I should think Rob's mind is on other things. Can't you call him?'

'Last time I tried, his mobile was switched off and I haven't got Tina's number.'

Mike frowned and I realised that my

emotions were written clearly on my face, all the stress of the last few weeks catching up with me, my fears about Rob and Tina. I swallowed.

'Oh, Karen. You think something's going on, don't you? Me and my big mouth. Look, for what it's worth, I don't think Rob would do the dirty on you. He's a decent bloke.'

'Then why hasn't he phoned?'

'Perhaps he's on his way back.'

'If I knew where from, I'd go and meet him.'

'Well, I can help you out on that one, too, as it happens. I know where Tina Marsh's place is. I could drive you down there.'

'But it's miles away. Haven't you got work to do?'

'There's nothing that can't wait. Anyway, I don't think you should be driving, the state you're in. It won't help matters if you end up in a hedge.'

'Are you sure you don't mind?' I heard my voice catching in my throat.

'No, I don't mind.' He grinned and

there was warmth in his face once more and fresh guilt swept through me. 'I could say, Karen, that it's what friends are for.'

★ ★ ★

We didn't talk much as we drove. Mike looked preoccupied and I was, too, all the pieces of the jigsaw dancing about in my head. Mike was right, Ben Darley might well have paid Lynne to move her horses. Putting us in financial difficulty could just swing our decision on whether or not to sell Shadowman, but the notes didn't fit in.

'The person who sent those notes wanted to ruin our marriage as well as our business,' I murmured, half to myself, half to Mike.

He nodded. 'They were pretty vindictive. From what I know about Ben, he's quite a ruthless man — which is why he's so successful at what he does — but I wouldn't have had him down as a vindictive one.'

'He wanted to buy Shadowman when he was a foal and Rob beat him to it. Maybe he's been stewing about that for all these years. Is that enough to make him want to split us up, do you think?'

'Who knows what goes on in people's heads? It's always puzzled me. Animals are far more straightforward. I shouldn't worry about it too much.' He glanced at me. 'We'll be there in about half an hour. How are you feeling?'

'Fine,' I said, which wasn't totally true. Unease was still churning away inside me. Why hadn't Rob rung me? He must know I'd be worried sick by now.

Twenty minutes later, Mike indicated to go down a narrow country lane, grey sheep dotting the fields on either side of us. 'How do you know where Tina lives?' I asked idly.

'I fancied her myself at one time.' Mike kept his eyes on the road, but there was a smile in his voice. 'She wasn't interested in me. I don't think she was interested in any man particularly. She was too tied up with horses.

She's done really well for herself, considering she started out with absolutely nothing. I quite admire her.'

'Talented as well as stunning then,' I said, feeling a little twist of jealousy and hoping it hadn't come out in my voice.

'More obsessive, I'd say. You'd have to be to get where she's got with no back-up and no money. She had a pretty rough upbringing. Her father did a bunk when she was little and her mother was a drunk.'

'She told you all this?'

'I read between the lines. She told me that she used to escape by going down to the riding stables and working in exchange for rides. The woman who owned it saw she had talent and took her under her wing. The only other person I've known who's ever got as far as Tina just on pure hard work and their riding ability is your Rob.'

'Sounds like they've got a lot in common,' I said quietly, but Mike didn't reply. He pulled into a gateway and I saw that our horsebox was parked beside a tatty caravan. So at least Rob was still here.

'Want me to wait here?' Mike said. 'Or would you rather I came in with you?'

I wanted him with me, but I wasn't at all sure of the reception I was going to get. His confidences about Tina had unsettled me a lot more than I wanted to admit. Maybe there was something in my parents' theory that couples with similar backgrounds had more chance of finding long-lasting love. Maybe that was at the bottom of Rob's distance. I didn't want to believe it, but I had to admit that I'd been worrying that Rob didn't feel as strongly as I did for weeks.

Was it intuition or paranoia, I wondered as I knocked on the front door? My intuition hadn't been too hot lately as far as everything else was concerned. I held on to this, listening to the sound of the doorbell reverberating through the house. No one came.

I turned back to the car, seeing that

Mike was watching me through the driver's window. A hedge ran round the house and there was also a dirt track, which looked as though it led through to another gate. Tina was probably out in the stables, which was why she wasn't answering the door. I hesitated. I didn't fancy just wandering about trying to find her, but it didn't look as though I had much choice. I was wavering about what to do when Mike got out of the car.

'Someone's in,' he said. 'I just saw the curtain move.' He crunched across the gravel towards me and I felt coldness clenching my stomach muscles. What was I going to do if Rob was having an affair with Tina? If all of the notes and the threats were part of some elaborate plan he'd cooked up to make me want to divorce him, to free him so he could be with Tina? I hugged my arms around myself, my heartbeat thundering in my head, my mouth dry with nerves.

'Come on,' Mike said, reading my face. 'Let's go and have a scout round.

Someone must be about.'

We were halfway down the track towards the gate when we heard a shout from behind us.

'Hey, where do you think you're going? This is private property.'

It was Tina, I saw, my stomach dropping away. She was dressed in jodhpurs and an old Barbour jacket, but her hair was loose and she looked beautiful. Insecurity fought with rationality and lost. There was no way Rob couldn't be tempted.

'I'm Karen Patterson,' I said quietly. 'I'm looking for my husband.'

'He's about somewhere.' She yawned and looked at Mike. 'Don't I know you?'

'We went out a few times — it was a long time ago,' he said.

'Well, it couldn't have been very memorable.' She looked back at me. 'You lot all sound the same to me, plummy accents, more money than you know what to do with. Don't know you've been born, half of you.'

I blinked, taken aback not so much at her words, but at the hostility in her eyes.

'That's not fair. You don't even know me.'

'I know you used your parents' money to buy a man who wouldn't have given you a second glance otherwise. Fancy a bit of rough, did you? Got tired of all your toffee-nosed boyfriends and wanted to try out a real man? Were you going to chuck him out after a few years when you got bored?'

I stared at her, hearing the poison in her voice, and suddenly all of Rob's insecurity about not being good enough for me made sense. She'd been feeding it to him, drip by drip.

And then Rob came round the corner, amazement spreading across his face. 'Karen, I've just been trying to get hold of you. What are you doing here?'

'You didn't phone.'

'I'm sorry, I didn't think about it. Shadowman had another bout of colic. I've been up all night with him.' He looked at Mike as if he was noticing him for the first time. 'You were right, I shouldn't have moved him. Is that why you've come? God, I'm sorry. I hope I haven't caused any permanent damage.' And he looked so tired and so vulnerable that it was all I could do to stop myself running across and hugging him.

'You've gone soft in your old age,' Tina said, giving him a look of contempt. 'That's what comes of marrying someone like her. You stop taking risks, get too comfortable. It's pathetic.'

I stepped towards her, everything slowly clicking into place. 'You're Well-wisher, aren't you? It's been you all along.'

She gave me a cold, bitter smile. 'Rob said you were pretty rattled. It's a mistake to get too complacent. Wrecks marriages, complacency.'

'Did you pay Lynne to move her horses?'

'I don't have that kind of money to

waste. No, that was Ben. He figured he'd soon get his money back if you sold him Shadowman.'

I was aware of Rob suddenly tuning in to this conversation. 'You deliberately gave my horse colic. You could have killed him.'

'I didn't touch your horse,' she said, suddenly angry. 'What do you take me for? I love horses.'

'But not people,' I said softly, so that only she could hear.

'Not people like you,' she spat, disdain in her blue eyes. 'If you hadn't come along, Rob and I would still be together.'

* * *

'I can understand her hating me enough to want to split us up,' I said to Rob, much later that day. 'But I really don't understand how she knew what was going on in our lives. Or how she managed to deliver the notes. They all came by hand.'

'I haven't got a clue. I didn't even know she felt like that about me. I'd always thought we were just good friends.'

'She was in love with you — she wouldn't have liked anyone you married, but when she found out it was me, it must have tipped her over the edge. Backgrounds are important to some people.'

'They are to your parents,' he said quietly. 'They've never thought I was good enough for you, have they?'

'Their main concern is that we're happy.' I squeezed his hand. 'And to be honest, I don't care what anyone else thinks — the only important thing is what we think. How we feel.'

'I'll second that,' he said, looking desperately tired. 'I'm sorry, Karen. I love you so much, but I've been worried sick these last few weeks. About money, about us, I just didn't know what to do for the best.'

'Well, I haven't been much better. I owe Mike an apology, too. I can't believe he's still speaking to me after I accused him of being Well-wisher.'

'Perhaps you should go round and see him, while I catch up on some sleep,' Rob said, yawning. 'Ask him round for dinner some time. He's a nice bloke.'

★　★　★

Mike said he'd be pleased to come to dinner. We chatted for a while about Tina and how she'd felt about Rob.

'Do you think she wanted to get me out of the picture so they could get back together?' I asked him.

'No, I think she just wanted to cause trouble. If she'd really cared about him, she wouldn't have wanted to hurt him. You don't try to hurt people who you care about. You're more likely to forgive them.' He reddened slightly as he spoke and I nodded, because I understood perfectly where he was coming from.

'Thanks, Mike, for everything,' I said again. 'If it hadn't been for you, Tina might have succeeded in splitting us up.'

'Yeah.' He gave me a smile full of irony. 'I must be completely mad.'

I swallowed and, as I turned away, he touched my shoulder. 'Don't suppose you fancy asking Hannah to dinner at the same time as me, do you? I think she's rather cute.'

'I'm sure it can be arranged,' I said happily.

★ ★ ★

We found out how Tina had known what was going on in our lives a few days later when another of our customers, Kathy, gave us a month's notice.

'I'm moving to Devon,' she said. 'I've a friend who runs a livery stables there — we used to go to school together. We met up at a reunion a couple of months ago and we've been in touch ever since.'

'I don't suppose her name's Tina Marsh?' I asked.

'That's right!'

'Did she ever give you any envelopes for us?' Rob added. 'Ask you to pop them through the door?'

'Yes, show schedules. She thought you might be interested. I told her you both competed.'

Rob and I exchanged glances, but we said no more. It was obvious that Kathy hadn't a clue what had been going on.

★   ★   ★

A couple of days later we were just about to get the horses in for the night when Mike called by. Rob told him about Kathy moving and he frowned.

'Of course I don't condone what Tina did, but she's going to need all the help she can get financially. I've just been to Ben Darley's place. He's none too pleased with Miss Marsh. In fact, they've fallen out about what she did to you, big time.'

'How did he know?' I asked, curious.

'Apparently Tina told him herself.

She expected him to be pleased, but he was horrified. They had a rather public row at some horse trials.'

'He wasn't exactly whiter than white himself,' Rob said wryly.

'True, but he wasn't out to destroy you. He just wanted to force your hand over Shadowman.' Mike hesitated. 'Tina doesn't own any really good horses. She's always ridden for Ben, but it doesn't look as if she will again. It will have quite a major impact on her career, I'd say.'

None of us said anything else. I couldn't say I got any satisfaction out of Mike's news. We hadn't wanted to press charges, not that we'd actually ever had any proof, but it seemed awfully harsh that Tina was about to lose all she really cared about. Condemned by her own bitterness. Reputation was everything in the horse world. And I knew what it was like to struggle financially.

'I hate to mention this again,' I said, when Mike had gone and Rob and I were walking down to the bottom field.

'But are we going to manage — what with losing another livery and no more seminars at Tina's?'

He grinned. 'I saw Lynne's dad yesterday. Apparently she's not too happy at Anne Gates' place. She thinks it's too big and impersonal and doesn't have the same atmosphere as here.'

'The same mystery and intrigue,' I said wryly.

'Something like that. Anyway, she was a bit embarrassed about what happened and didn't like to ask if she could come back, so I phoned her. And to cut a long story short, she's moving back at the end of the month.'

'You're wonderful.'

His fingers closed around mine. 'Told you I wouldn't let you down, didn't I?'

We'd reached the edge of the field where Shadowman was grazing with the other horses. The sun was just setting beyond the trees, so that the nearest ones looked as though they were on fire, their leaves flaming red. The place had never looked so beautiful, perhap because for the first time in months I felt secure and tentatively optimistic about the future.

I glanced at Rob's peaceful face and thought how wrong Tina had been. I'd never been complacent about our marriage, quite the opposite, but the past few weeks had helped to put things in perspective. Made me see what was important and what wasn't.

When we got closer to the horses, we could see two kids were standing by the fence, rustling bread bags.

'Hey,' Rob called to them. 'Scarper, you two. These horses have enough to eat. They don't need extras.'

I put my hand on his arm. 'Wait a minute.' Then I turned towards the elder of the kids. 'Have you fed them anything before? Have you ever given them apples?'

The boy stared back at me, his face mutinous. 'Might have done. What's it to you?'

'Why don't you come up to the tables one day?' I said, softening my voice. 'You could maybe have a ride on a horse and we could teach you about what they can eat and what they can't.'

He nodded.

'You're crazy,' Rob said as we led Shadowman and the other horses back in for the night. 'That's how Tina started off — and look where she ended up. They were a right pair of ruffians, those two.'

'It's how you started, too,' I reminded him. 'And don't be so judgmental. Backgrounds have nothing to do with how we turn out. It's the person inside who counts.'

'Bit of a risk, though, isn't it?' He took my hand and kissed it.

'I happen to think some risks are worth taking,' I said, and kissed him back.

We do hope that you have enjoyed reading this large print book.

Did you know that all of our titles are available for purchase?

We publish a wide range of high quality large print books including:
Romances, Mysteries, Classics
General Fiction
Non Fiction and Westerns

Special interest titles available in large print are:
The Little Oxford Dictionary
Music Book, Song Book
Hymn Book, Service Book

Also available from us courtesy of Oxford University Press:
Young Readers' Dictionary
(large print edition)
Young Readers' Thesaurus
(large print edition)

For further information or a free brochure, please contact us at:
Ulverscroft Large Print Books Ltd.,
The Green, Bradgate Road, Anstey,
Leicester, LE7 7FU, England.
Tel: (00 44) **0116 236 4325**
Fax: (00 44) **0116 234 0205**

Other titles in the
Linford Romance Library:

FLIGHTS OF FANCY

Sheila Holroyd

Jessica always does the sensible thing — until she meets James Strang . . . In Prague with friends, Jessica is grateful when a bag thief is foiled by James' intervention. Back home, although James lives in Birmingham and Jessica in Manchester, she finds herself agreeing to help James in his hour of need, and turning to him in hers. So when he suddenly vanishes from her life, Jessica is hurt and bewildered. Should she have just played it safe after all?

MISS SHAW AND THE DOCTOR

Fenella Miller

Sarah Shaw, on her way to take up a position as governess with Lady Fenwick, accidentally causes Dr Adam Moorcroft to be thrown from his gig and over the hedge — not an auspicious start to their relationship. When Isobel Fenwick contracts measles, Sarah moves her charges to Adam's home to protect the new-born Fenwick heir. However, tragedy strikes . . . Sarah promises she will stay as long as the girls need her. But will she be able to keep her promise?